N.L. Tim II

Kevin C. McLeod, MD

WESTBOW
PRESS®
A DIVISION OF THOMAS NELSON
& ZONDERVAN

WestBow Press books may be ordered through booksellers or by contacting:

WestBow Press
A Division of Thomas Nelson & Zondervan
1663 Liberty Drive
Bloomington, IN 47403
www.westbowpress.com
844-714-3454

ISBN: 979-8-3850-0563-5 (sc)
ISBN: 979-8-3850-0564-2 (e)

Library of Congress Control Number: 2023908995

Print information available on the last page.

WestBow Press rev. date: 08/21/2023

CONTENTS

N.L. and His Snowman

Back in those days along CCC the best weatherman was a Grandpa who could walk out from the front porch look skyward, feel something in the breeze, taste something in the wind, watch a bird fly, see what the cows were doing then turn around and declare, 'norther will blow by 3 AM, temperature will drop 25 degrees and snow will commence mid morning for sure.'

On his over -sight alone extra wood would be piled, mules and horses would be stabled, more hay thrown into feed troughs, and dogs and cats accommodated inside the plank wood house that leaked chilled air like a flour sifter.

There was really only two warm places in the house by the fireplace or Mrs. Ella's wood burning stove any place else was Canada. Long Johns, extra socks, mittens, head scarf, and a hot water bottle crisscrossed up under the sheets was the only way to start off going to bed.

N.L.'s loft room was an igloo and he was the only one to get the extra hot water bottle to snuggle up to. He disappeared under 3 of Mrs. Ellas hand woven blankets to hibernate the night with the teeth of ice cycles grinning just outside his frosted window.

Now if it did snow like Grandpa said he was dreaming to build the best snowman ever. He saw in his mind's eye the big base belly, mounded chest, round head with a cucumber nose, charcoal eyes, straw hair with top hat.

Next morning it was very cold, his breathing blew out fog as he dressed for school. No snow had fallen yet so it was business as usual. An ice pick wind impaled the windshield as Pete in the model T chugged along taking the bundled kids to school.

Their teacher there allowed an arrangement of desks circling the black iron furnace. Then just afore noon just like Grandpa said little white flakes started pirouetting in swirls growing to drifting dimes and in flurries silver dollar dragoons. Like a giant artist with only a pastel of white ol'man winter coated the land in cream. Over each wire, post top, fence rail, tree branch, got a dazzle line of icey purity.

They decided to end school at 1 PM to get kids home before the worst of the coming tundra. Some waited at the school, others decided to adventure on home. N.L. started out his boots sinking into the crunching snow, he felt like a pioneer leaving his trail clearly marked behind. The cold started crawling up under his jacket like a thief stealing heat from his pockets.

He was surprised when his friend Toby came galloping by on his horse, 'Hey N.L. grab this rope I'll pull ya home!' The rope tied around the saddle horn had a loop on the trailing end and N.L. grabbed a hold. At first he was skidding, almost skiing (though he had never skied before)). He braced his boots ahead allowing himself to sled style slide along behind.

The speed seemed to increase his boots were swerving first right then left with snow being plowed up all over him. He wanted to let go but by now his coat and gloves were twisted up in the loop.

Toby looking back thought N.L. was towing along just fine cause the constant snowfall was blinding his eyes also. 100 yards away from home N.L. skipped sideways and down he plunged, being dragged along now like a log. He tried to yell to Toby to 'STOP!' but snow balls and clods kicked from the horse's hooves drowned out any shouting.

Somehow Pete and Mrs. Ella had heard something and were out on the front porch where Toby halted with 'whoa!' his horse. Slowly out of a snow pile rose a staggering, dazed, blinded, snowman or snowboy for he was covered head to boot. Snow was caked inside his jacket and jeans and boots. He spewed snow out of his mouth, blew snow out of his nose, wiped snow from his eyes and ears. Toby trying not to laugh shouted over, 'wont me to stay over and help you build that snowman you were talking about?'

N.L. rolled up snow from inside his jacket into a ball and though he could not be sure exactly where Toby was he tossed it in his general direction. Mrs. Ella ran out, 'Oo N.L. we'll get to the fireplace right now!' Pete kept his grinning under his handkerchief watching his boy walk like his jeans were frozen columns with a polar bear suit above. Pete holler out to Toby.' best go on home now looks like N.L.s had all the snowmaning he can take for one day!"

N.L. AND PETE'S TRACTOR

Back in 1919 on CatClaw Creek Pete got his last child, the baby boy N.L. and the next year the largest cash crop of his farming career. Cotton prices after WWI went sky-high and the fickleness of nature favored every foot of their farm with the largest brighter whitest bulbs this side of Egypt.

With this yield Pete put in for Mrs. Ella a new kitchen stove and ice box plus a closed back porch. .He sold his mules for a machine- a blue Ford tractor and for the rest of his life he tried to match that boomer year of hardwork to profit. As N.L. was growing up Pete would tell him 'now there's 32 horses working in that there machine!' N.L. walked all around that tractor and never saw a hoof, or mane, or any kind of leather-reins, harness, halters. He surmised that with that many horses in there better add extra bags of oats to the gas.

When N.L. got to be 6 years old he was Pete's best fetcher- by frame of body and mind. Pete would say that a barefooted N.L. could out scoot a road-runner in sneakers. He was often called for runs back to house or barn or shed for wrenches, rope, sandwiches, nails, water, bandages.

Now unknown to anybody Homer by the ol hook or crook method got a 1920 Indian scout motorcycle and was able to hide it in the barn behind a haystack waiting for just the right moment to demonstrate it to Pete and Ella his good fortune.

His best thought was to wait for a sunday morning and ride it to church. His 'savior-scooter' with religious intent might be just the righteous angle needed.

Homer had also been sold the idea of 'additives' that would give extra mileage and power out of the scooter. He kept this high octane brew in a gas can it too hidden among the hay. On this hot summer day some of the dogs scratched out for themselves a hay padded bed to find that certain cool spot in the barn, thus uncovering the gas can.

N.L. had already made several jogging trips in order to fetch things for Pete. Pete yelled, 'son now we need a little more fuel to finish the day, go get that can of diesel will ya-thanks!' It was not easy lugging that heavy can all the way back out to the fence line. When he got back down there, Elmer had followed and Pete down the fence line a ways was checking on a post hollered,' Elmer -you and N.L. pour that can in there.'

They did as instructed. When Homer stepped out of the barn he realized his can was gone and he could see where. But it was too late to stop the 'additive!'

Pete climbed back on and the tractor roared off as usual much to Homer's fleeting relief. Then all of sudden there was a massive jerk and booming back fire as Pete rode a metal Burmah bull. Black soot cannoned out of the stove pipe with the tractor bellowing like a wounded dinosaur then a final 'BOOM!'"

Down climbed Pete looking like a Pennsylvania coal miner directing his charge to the startled N.L.. 'what in blue blazes did you put in that tractor?'

N.L. stammered 'like you told me PaPa the diesel, the red can.'

'Red can? Red- there is no RED CAN!' and Pete could tell Elmer did not know anything a miss. Looking up to the barn Pete saw Homer standing there statue like, he waved and hollered for him to come down there. "Homer let's have it!' The 'surprise' scooter with additive story came all out with a 'don't that beat the band!' summation on Pete's face. Homer did get to ride his scooter, though- only once back into town for a re-sale.

They drained the gas lines and got pure diesel back in and she came back to a more healthy purring puttering sound. Years later during WW2 N.L. was back home on leave, Mr. Pete and Mrs. Ella were out on the front porch. Said Pete,'son on your way back out could you bring us all some more tea?'

It was not a minute that he returned with a tumbler of iced tea with lemons. Pete put on a smile thinking from the past asking,' Son yu sure this doesn't have any of the 'additives' in it?'

N.L. Comes Into The World

Old timers said the summer of 1919 was the most parched as ever in West Texas and the few Indians who lived in little houses along CatClaw Creek said they could not remember when the tongues of buffalo hung so low.

Mrs. Ella was baring through these dog-days with her 10th pregnancy. In her 9 previous deliveries she had borne 5 boys-three and one set of twins, and then 5 girls. This last baby would tip the scales.

Legend has it that to influence the cause the boys had put a baseball bat up under Pete and Ella's bed. And the girls not to be outdone put a Sears & Roebuck catalog opened to the forbidden
'Section' * behind the head board.

August was nearly gone but still the heat hung over everything like a giant woolen horse-blanket.

Mrs. Ella awoke suddenly in the middle of the night saying,' Pete could you fetch me some kinda cool water?' Instead of his feet landing on the bare boarded floor that bat had rolled out, he stepped down, and he did a ½ somersault before sprawling out beside the bed.. A great sustained moan drafted thru the house and when the lone electric light was flicked on there were children in bed clothes standing in the door way and Pete in long-johns trying to realign hips, knees, and ankles.

Mrs. Ella got tickled and more so when little snickers came upon the children's faces as well. No one saw his fall but it was the geriatrics and facial contortions of the aftermath that got them in a matinee mood. Mrs. Ella was about finished with her bout when suddenly she stopped in mid-smile,

'Pete, Pete- now this may be something-now listen it's gonna be alright but go get Dr. Baker-ok'

Pete whirled around seeing Charlton (the oldest), 'Charlton! I'll stay here you take the Model-T and go get Doc Baker!' Girls ya'll gather around Mama and fan her! I'll go get that water.'

With so many drinkers in the house the kitchen water bucket was bone dry so he carried it and ran barefooted out the back door covering the red dusty ground to the well. Trying to sit the kitchen bucket down on the rim he accidentally knocked it over the edge, instinctively he quickly reached down to save it at the same time putting his other hand up on the cross bar. Cross bars are designed for weighted water buckets but not a man's weight hanging down now at the top of the well. The cracked piece hit him on the head causing a small bleed but he was able to frog leg a hold to keep from falling down into that dark abyss. He still had the kitchen bucket in hand but the pulley, rope, and wheel bucket were down that hole.

The gossamer moon was reluctantly and stingingly showing a

wisp of glow just enough to keep everything in shadow. He needed rope for the bucket now quick walking to the barn his bare feet found every burr left on the ground. On the side wall he could make out some rope pegged up there but not seeing the horses shoes they dislodged and fell directly down on his toes, scraping skin with a bleed.

He could short-cut through a side door which was usually closed and when he did he was captured in strings of spider webs criss-crossing his face. Back to the well he quickly tied the rope on to the kitchen bucket and let it fall hearing the splash. Pulling up the bucket it was ready to clear the well's rim when he mis-handled the handle and spilled over half that load on his long-johns. So back down goes the bucket with a better pull up this time.

Then he stopped something told him to be still and listen, all was quite, he did not move, waited-then he heard it - the baby's first cry! "Whoppee!" he exclaimed running back to the house sloushing more water out of the bucket but he did not care. He did not stop till at the bedroom door, inside he saw it, Mama and the girls were fussing over this tiny pink bundle with blinking eyes.

Gratefully looking up Mrs. Ella said, 'well Pete you boys done won out come see your baby boy.' Pete could only shuffle his sore feet still holding on to the bucket. Mrs. Ella said, 'why I sure will take that drink now' Pete was going to hand her the whole bucket when he asked,' but you, you, are you OK?'

Returned Ella, 'fine, just fine husband.' (which was the only time she ever called him that)-special.

About that time Carlton with Dr. Baker rushed into the room. In a matter of minutes Dr. Baker was backing out of the room saying to Pete, "mama's fine, baby is fine." Then he looked at Pete with blood dried on his head and feet, spider webs clinging everywhere, straw in his hair, wet long-johns, bruised face and said, "Ella did all the delivery but looks like you had the worst of labor pains!' As if to say an 'Amen' the new little boy baby made a small cry that echoed through the house and thankfully Pete got for himself a celebration drink of well deserved well-water!

- The Section was the pages showing women's under garments.

N.L. Gets a New Ice Box

In the summer of '25 some would say it was blue blazes hot in West Texas and only a side step away from the devil's own kitchen. Rooster spit was gone so there were no cockadoodaldoo's, young couples stopped sparking on account of the fire hazard, and the only water in CatClaw Creek was mirage water. The cool water was on the northside of Pete and Ella's rock rimmed inground well. This always bewildered N.L. seeing that the water bucket would always drop straight down but sometimes Pete would come in the kitchen.' Ella you'll like this water, had to break ice along the wells north wall to get it!' Ella always smiled a little.

As Lucifer must have ordained it himself the old ice box put out a rickety rusted bottom and died. Nothing to do but call the Merkel mercantile over the party phone and order a new one. It would turn out to be a White Mountain wood stained deep freezing double squared ice block holding box complete with an installation man on arrival to the kitchen's back door.

Now discussion about this arctic wonder was ticklin the children but it seemed Homer knew more about chillin and frostin than anybody. Yet he only let N.L. in on his final secret wisdom. Homer whispered to N.L.' now they say afore anything gets put in it like this new one coming that words spoken into it will freeze in midair and later if you open the door long enough they'll thaw and bark right out of the box!' 'OK,' gulped the big eyed N.L.

Thereafter the great day soon arrived. The installation man was busy with the set-up when the front door was knocked upon by relatives. The house hold ran up front except for N.L. and the installation man who by now had two huge blocks of ice placed inside. In getting the door closed he dropped a wrench onto his gout afflicted great toe. There was a discharge of a torrent blue sure to be spankin 'words as the man shut the door.

In a small shock N.L. was left alone with the knowledge that those Delila words were frozen up inside. Very soon Pete and Ella and the relatives all came back to admire the White Mountain box.

Said Mrs. Ella, 'O'Pete I can't wait to feel the chill that's gonna be in there!'

Returned Mr. Pete, 'well you might need to wait a bit and let it get that way first.'

N.L. positioned himself over the front door with arms crossed, 'no mama you can't open her now or maybe ever!' That sure put people back on their heels and he continued,' only a preacher Isuppose can do it right.'

Pete was smiling, 'well son we've got a preacher right here!' (That was Elmer's twin brother Delmer nicknamed 'preacher' cause he was

always going about asking for 'contribution' money.) Now N.L. said'
no paw i mean a real one out of church!'

Pete said, 'now son we've heard enough!'

'No you haven't' declared N.L.

Pete stated,' now you stand back I'm gonna open her up now'.

N.L. asked him to just wait then he motioned for Mrs Ella to lean down alittle so he could cup her ears. Pete got a hold of the handle and the new door was jammed so he gave an extra tug when he did the top block of ice slide out and landed square on his stocking feet. Pete's face went purple and through clenched teeth he mumbled, 'I'm going out to the barn!' They could all hear from there the muffled damnations and the Thou Shalt Nots spewing forth.

N.L. took his hands away and said to Mrs. Ella,'sure glad Dad took those bad words out of here and out to the barn where they belong!' Mrs. Ella smiled a little with a head nog.

N.L. Gets His First Pair of Shoes

Now when Mrs. Ella finally gave birth to her last child she was in her mid-thirties and Dr. Baker said.

'Now this is probably the last 'hooraw'. Speculations from the cousins was that with N.L. born so far down the line that he was only the rankings and scrapings and might not be fit for any work other than maybe in the Barnum & Bailey circus.

As time went on Mrs. Ella kept N.L. close by plus all the older sisters fussed over him, practiced their eventual own motherhood skills on him, and would have him to 'tea'. He learned that girls played soft games like bean bag toss and worked puzzles while the boys would throw rocks and try to ride bareback the farm animals.

Almost everything he got was 'army issue' seeing that an older sibling had already marched with it.

At age 8 and just starting school he got from Homer a pair of' religious' oxfords. Called that because the soles were 'holy' and were 'saved' by a piece of sandal leather prayerfully inserted inside the toe box.

N.L. did not mind the issue anyway cause his own bare feet were tougher than mule leather and had served him well running everywhere over prickly ground. He actually had speed with those feet, plus mesquite tree climbing or running along the muddy bottom of Cat Claw Creek.

They were late in delivery but Mrs. Ella and Pete had already ordered some lace up ankle toppers that were brown leather. N.L. had heard in church that in Heaven we would all get a robe and crown, and new sandals but for now he just soon as wait on any divine duds. As it turned out he only had to wear the ill-fitting Homer oxfords for 2 days cause when he came home there on the front porch was a parcel box wrapped in twine with his name on it-'N.L. McLeod.'

At first he was alot more interested in the box itself but seeing the pleading faces of Pete and Ella he got the box opened. There arose the most sweet appealing fresh leather aroma that demanded a nose dive into the wrapping paper. Finally the shods came out in perfection of newness, pristine, altar sacrificing- these shoes he thought should only be offered up to God. They were the real religion. They gleaned up to him, reflecting a shine, and his jaw dropped, he was a mute.

Next day he started out squeaky with the new leather but as soon as he got to walking where Pete and Ella could not see, he took them off reverently tying the shoe strings together he slung them over his shoulder. Up the road some men were at work putting up a new telephone line across the lane and one of them could not help this comment.'Hey sonny dem shoes will walk a whole lot better on your feet instead of your shoulders!' That got a big laugh from his crew.

There was a big kid 'Mackey' who lived up in town and he saw this going on a couple of days and bumping into N.L. said.'hey don't you know your shoes from mittens- shoes are suppose to carry us not us carry them you knuckle head!' N.L. had his plans and returned.'mind your own beeswax.'

This did not appease big Mackey and he said,'if'n I ever see you out carrying dem shoes I'm gonna take' em and whoop you good-hear!

For the next few days N.L. kinda slid around staying out of sight. Then this evening N.L. got detention for talking in class and the teacher left on an errand telling him, 'beat all the chalk out the erasers-I'll be back.' That was OK with N.L. cause he wanted everybody to clear out anyway. When the teacher finally came back she said,' N.L. ? you still here? Get on home it's getting late!'

N.L. gathered up his new shoes and took his bare feet out to the gravel road for the ½ mile walk back home. Lost in thought he suddenly felt a whoosh! coast by him and it was big Mackey on this bicycle, 'Hold on you!' N.L. heard him as he slid his tires to turn around. Quick as a camera shutter N.L. had to do something with those shoes so he gave them the best high toss he could hoping they would land out somewhere for him to find later. Mackey was sorely disappointed to find N.L. shoeless and so let him go with a shove. Now N.L. looked all over in the gathering dark, both sides of the road, beyond the road, in the fields-gone!? Vanished-gone!?

Of course when he got home Pete and Ella wanted to know where his new shoes were. N.L.s only explanation was,' reckon the Lord needed 'm up in heaven.' Explaining that he had to toss them skyward and they never came back down. He was sent to bed without supper to think over why 'the Lord would need his shoes worse than he did.' Next morning there arose a bewildered world, especially the telephone men for there strung over the new line hung spit-polished new shoes!

Word of such shot down to the McLeod house when all eyes turned to N.L.. He shrugged,' well all I know is that the Lord may only want sandals and not shoes !!' The telephone men were able to snatch the shoes off the line and were waiting when Pete drove N.L. down there. Pete had told him to apologize for interfering with their work and he did. Said one of them.'well son we knew they weren't gonna help you get about up on our wire. So if you'll just wear them on your feet we won't have to come to their rescue anymore. We'll let this time go and no one has to foot the bill!'

N.L. learns about Marriage

One afternoon in the McLeod kitchen N.L. was on duty helping Mrs. Ella and Pete hand wash, dry, wipe clean and stack up dishes from a big Sunday family meal. The meal (post church of course) was always ravishly attended by aunts, uncles, and their various cousins from up and down CatClaw Creek.

This sunday after lunch a sundry of options saturated the home—rest out on the porch, curl up on a couch, spread one's self on a pallet, or more formally take to bed. No one ever exclaimed it or pronounced it but in the McLeod home the LORD's day was a rest-day. Only thing left going with any tempo was the radio which was allowed to waft through the front rooms like a floating newspaper page. King George V was ruling England and the program was a reenactment of his royal wedding.

The radio announcer in full cockney dialect with a mental brush and pallet with strokes and dabs of speech - painted before them the full formality of the court, the regal regalia of princesses, frocks of groomsmen, parade horses and carriages. The charmed broadcaster unfolded the pageantry like a huge flower petal by petal whisked away and blown over the airwaves to the far reaches of the realm even to west Texas!

Finishing the kitchen chores Pete's suspenders wear down and he was dressed in under shirt and trousers. Mrs.Ella took her apron off, kicking out of her solid heel shoes, and N.L was already bare chested and footed looking for a nap. In contrast to the plumes of the announcer this was about as Camelot as West Texas gets.

Weddings were thru Neiman Marcus way back in Dallas or read about in story books, not one of N.L.'s brothers or sisters even had one. Mrs. Ella and Pete had eloped down in Bald Prairie, Texas one night in the 1894 with most of their children doing the same or just showing up from the Justice of the Peace with matrimonial papers. So when N.L. turned around to his parents and asked 'what's a wedding?' they both at first just had to look at each other. Composure came and Pete began, 'well son this is biblical, before you get two pages into the good book you have one a marriage that is. The Lord himself performed the first marriage giving Miss Eve to Mr. Adam.' Added Mrs. Ella,' and it was a garden wedding so it must have been garlanded and grand with animals all around.' And in the end Pete said,' God created it so His people could multiply, be fruitful and have just what we have here today-family!' They also explained about the elopement they had cause their families were just too poor to try to host a full scale 'wedding.'

This all seemed to hold N.L.'s mind for the moment.

Next day at school some of the children had heard the same broadcast and the girls especially were excited about the floral festivities described and if a white-horsed knight might someday ride in for them. N.L. explained that no one in his family had gone thru such poppycock.. And said as he understood it, 'it's all in the Bible you're to be fruitflies and go cantaloupe!'

Years later in 1942 with the world at war, WW II, on both sides of America and themselves N.L.Tim and Burnya Mae McHam (after sitting in ACC chapel knee to knee) would be the only one out of Mrs. Ella and Pete's 11 children to have a formal wedding. It was held at the McHam home 2014 Collins Avenue in Wichita Falls. He was in his dress U.S.Army Aircorps uniform and she was in suit dress with hat. They would remain married for the next 58 years-royally!

N.L. LEARNS SPIDERS

Out on Cat Claw Creek in west Taylor County Pete and Ella got a visit from the Blackmons- Mrs. Ella's parents from the black land of Franklin County, Bald Prairie, east Texas. Paps Blackmon had a 'war between the states' pension and together with Grams Blackmon they raised all their own food. They hauled in bushels of large eared corn, beets, purple hulled peas, tomatoes, green peppers-varieties that did not grow worth a bean in the red dust near Trent.

N.L. was fascinated with this plunder from the land as bushel baskets stacked up on the back porch to look like a fully stocked market. Grams Blackmon and he (as he was being shown) were shucking the corn when he pulled up an ear that had a black speckled spider looking to spit poison in his eye. Homer had schooled him on the wiles of death spitting spiders.

He was looking for a way to get Grams to smash it for him when she reached over calm as the cucumber in the next bushel and gently grasped the spider in her hand.

"O gram you'd best hammer him!' shouted N.L.

Grams calmly replied,'now darling dats just a baby O'Mr. Garden spidey, he's good bug catching, sides he has his ways of making God's world better.' With that she tossed him out the screen door.

Grams took N.L. walking around the house and barn and showed him knowledge about spiders. She said.

'Back home if it tweren't for dirt dobbers and spider webs our sheds would have blown down long ago!'

She showed him under an old sitting bucket.'now looky here for this one, dis is a devil, Mrs. Blackwidow- she's about the onlyest one you gotta mind to.

She can hurt awful and get you real sick. Reckon we gotta send her on her way.' Grams smacked her dead with the heel of her shoe and still holding her shoe she spoke over it to N.L. 'See she like hiding out, old places, under logs, just you know what your grabbin when your grabbin and you'll likely be alright.'

From then on he made a point to show Grams all the spiders about and what he had learned from her spider ways that even the webs make a good patch for a fresh wound like a medicine. Now it was time for N.L. to return back to fall school. First day teacher had all the children cleaning and sweeping since the rooms had been idle all summer. Suddenly there was a commotion. Someone said,'Becky don't move- this is no joke- there is a spider on your back!' Becky wanted to scream but she stood dead still, 'just get it off!' Even the teacher was perplexed not knowing whether to 'shoo or swat.'

N.L. could see that this spider was a fly catcher and no harm to anybody. So reaching out he scooped it with a secure snatch right into his hand. He heard exclamations, 'Smash it! Throw it down! Did you kill it?-kill it! Someone get a broom!' N.L. did not pay them any mind but as cool as salted ice he calmly walked out the door followed at at distance by some of the boys. The teacher and girls were looking over the nearly fainted Becky for other critters.

N.L. turned around getting outside,"now you all get back, I'm gonna let this one go and you aint gonna know where cause you'd probably chunk rocks at it or something- now get back inside before i toss it on you!' The boys went to looking out the windows as N.L. roamed the yard acting like you do playing nibble in the under water when you let go the stick. No one even went out later to even look for that spider and for the rest of that day N.L. was given a wide curve and open road.

He did not know it at the time but this started a little ember of curiosity about God's creatures. This slowly became a flare then a life-long flame when he graduated as an animal doctor from the veterinary class at Texas A&M '49. He connected the links back to his beloved Gram Blackmon and her spider knowing ways. Knowledge takes the 'mist' out of mystery.

N.L.'s First Christmas
on CatClaw Creek

When N.L. was born August 1919 Christmas was still 4 months away but his parents and 10 older siblings certainly knew that this one was going to be special- the last child for Pete and Ella would be THE BABY! in the house.

When the time came a cedar tree nailed into crossed boards was in the corner living room decorated with ribbons, popcorn strings, the silver tinseled star was yet to be placed on the top branch.

That winter a trick norther blew straight across the high plains driving snow upon the windows such that the house became a drift catcher all along the north porch. The front door was deemed 'shut!' because any opening would allow an imagery Yukon dog slid into the house.

Just the same Pete and the boys keep the fireplace stoked carrying the wood thru the house from the back door and most of the smoke did curl up the chimney. No matter when Christmas morning came and Pete and Ella had their coffee cups steaming they gave the go-ahead and there was a wild scramble of kids of all ages to find the brown wrapped present with their name on it under the tree. Strewn over the floor like a geologic sediment was the yule tide discharges oldest to youngest.

To the surprise of all, that froze all this action came a series of knocks from the front door. Looking out of the frosted windows they could just make the man's form, it was their neighbor and postman Old Jenkins. When he had finished his deliveries the day before covered over by snow in the bottom of his buggy was this package addressed to: N.L. McLeod from Franklin, Texas in Robertson County the home of Ella's parents, the Blackmons. The package recipient was content enough in his basket on the floor to let the older ones handle this and not have it bother his morning nap.

Pete was able to open a window while snow swirled thru to tell Old Jenkins to go to the back door.

Turning around the whole herd of them rambled out to go through the kitchen. Pete was excited himself and thought he had secured the window. He was surprised that Old Jenkins would mush out in this blizzard storm for such an errand. He wanted to invite him in for hot coffee, which was offered and excepted with good cheers all around.

Then Mrs. Ella realized that baby N.L was still up in the front room, 'Pete the baby boy!' This turned the whole parade stamping back thru the house to find the window wide open, snow, papers, wrappings, boxes everywhere. Pete literally dove into the pile hollering,' Homer close that window!'

A group of groundhogs could not have performed a better job of heaping up the debris, papers flying up, boxes thrown aside, finally from under the land fill came a joyful cheer from Pete 'Got Him!'

N.L's. little body was raised above the tide of tinsel for Mrs. Ella to see. She said 'O give him to me I'll warm him up!'

Remembering the package Pete opened it up saying 'well now this ought to do the task!' He produced a hand knitted baby blanket, cap, mittens, and booties saying 'he'll toast up like a backlog now!' When Mrs. Ella got him all suited up he looked like a little snow child. Everyone remembered that Christmas as the one when N.L. became a snowman in his own house.

N.L.'s Halloween and the Talking Jack-O-Lantern

In Taylor County, Texas along CatClaw Creek October became long-sleeves and full trouser weather wear. Also, it meant the arrival of bushels of crisp apples and pumpkins hauled in from east Texas.

Mrs. Ella would harvest all the innards including grinding up the seeds for her pumpkin pies and fried turnovers, leaving the shells for carving and decoration a few days before Halloween.

The thing about pumpkins is that each face is a novelty bearing the touch of the carver. N.L. envisioned a gapped tooth smiling semi-scarey mug as he commenced to curve.

He was confined to Mrs. Ella's back porch, where she said 'now know this is one fine kitchen sharp knife-be mindful-rule it with a smooth stroke, it's hard pushing on a dull one that will cut ye!'

First, he curved wild wide eyes and then a lopsided toothy grin that if applied properly might back a bear down out of a tree David Crockett style. About finished he heard his Mama calling him back in to help place the evening supper dishes. Unknown to N.L. him leaving the porch allowed a young hoot-owl an opening to perch on a branch of the mesquite tree just beside the back stairs.

Moments later N.L. returned to admire his craving, rearing back shouted out,'you do look great!' It was then that the pumpkin came to life asking, 'who, who?' He grabbed his chin and softly gave it out again,'you look great!' evoking the face before him to respond 'who, who?' Now he knew for sure and ran back into the kitchen, "Mama. Mama come see my pumpkin talks!'

Mrs. Ella looked up from her stirring pot, well what did it say?" N.L. answered, 'who, who.' Return Mrs. Ella, 'your pumpkin of course, what did it say?'

'Well mama it was kinda a 'who, who' question,"

'You go get that thing and bring it here,' she instructed.

By now the hoot-owl had flown away, however something else was astir, a prairie mouse was on the back porch and had scampered into the pumpkin head. N.L. gathered his pumpkin up under arm and back inside sat it down on the table 'now just listen Mama he'll talk.' They both leaned in a little, Mrs. Ella doing so to bemuse her son, and just for a minute all was silent till out came a distinct, 'Tweek, tweek.'

Mrs. Ella reacted like a hornet stung horse!, 'Pete! Pete!' She was back peddling with skid marks over the floor.

Now Mrs. McLeod was one seasoned and stalwart Bald Prairie breed Texas woman who could out grin polecats, ring tailed foxes, even snakes but for the family Rodentia she had only skin crawling seizures. Pete came bounding into the kitchen instinctively grabbing a broom with Mrs. Ella pointing wildly at the pumpkin exclaiming, "that pumpkin squeaked!'

When Pete opened the capped off portion of the pumpkins head all three jumped in different directions as out sprung the mouse, launched out with a sailing as if airborne, a great impersonation of a flying squirrel. Pete swung with the broom, the back swing jarring the ceiling's naked light bulb causing it to twirl about Hitchcock psycho style. As the light strobed, flash, dark, flash, dark their tabby cat watched the whole scene intently from the corner of the room, braced but collected with the humans scurrying around then-DASH as quick as a bat-wings beat she jumped over the table and captured the mouse prancing off with it as if she was just been coronated queen of England. That Halloween N.L. sure brought excitement into the McLeod home along CatClaw Creek with his talking pumpkin.

N.L. Becomes a Knight for a Day

With CatClaw Creek twisting down below the Mesa'a base and after a saturday movie matinee of watching Ivanhoe it was easy for N.L. to look up to the blue hill-tops envisioning castles rimming the heights, their massive shadows gliding out over their little farm. Here his serf-parents and sibling peasants lived in a humble cottage. BUT! His quest was to rise above these stockades and become a heralded plumed knight of the realm!

For the moment he would have to use sway-backed Tobe as his stead and the dusty barn tack while he imagined a pinion charger with head guard and rampant lion draped saddle. Actually medieval armor was hard to come by in Trent, Texas without true established feudalism.

This new challenge forN.L. required a new language so he started using out of the King James Bible the host of thee's and thou's which was still allowable in open prayers but not in conversation. He would throw out therefores and hath nots which everybody mostly ignored except for Homer who using the same vernacular called him a 'knave.' N.L. figured a knave was a good start to beginning a knight's quest and let the remark go without throwing down a glove (rather gauntlet).

The barn with a new arrangement of hay bales become his first stronghold and the loft ladder his drawbridge, all easily defended by one knight's solitaire dedication. Among debris in the non-burnable pile he found his helmet, sure it had been a cook pot before now with leather straps underneath and blue bird feathers taped above it became regal head gear. A tin sign 'You-Need-A-Biscuit' turned around became his breastplate. He rolled old tin foil over Tobe's reins and the saddle prommel to give them a look of chivalry. Mrs.Ella gave him a blotched old bed sheet for his saddle drape transforming Tobe into a heavy horse of an ancient calvary.

There were no swords in the mercantile and Pete did not trust him with the machete, so N.L. whittled down a broomstick to become his lance-o-doom. The day came gathering all this up for his first (and only) tournament upon his charger: N.L. Esquire McLeod O'Trent. Without any royal announcement, nor posted posters, bugles, or long trumpets he decided to practice his new calling jousting down the lane between Mrs. Ella's clothes lines.

The west Texas winds surely can billow Mrs. Ella's fresh washed sheets giving the grounds pageantry. Aside the barn N.L. had already unhorsed about a dozen adversaries running Tobe, a stead of speed, even though it was more of a high gear trot. Homer was the only one lurking about who had actually watched any of this heroics and had seen enough. Homer positioned himself around the outhouse out of sight to the 'knight'. N.L. was realigning Tobe for another tilt alongside the barn when Homer with sling-shot in hand pulled back and let fly a well aimed marble directly onto Toby's rear. Tobe reared and wheeled around and pall-mall bolted in an erratic whirl right at the clothes line.

The knight was gathering leather trying to stay saddled with helmet eschew, lance whipping Tobe's head, his drape sheet blowing up before his viser as they ran the line. Now the lance was skewering Mrs. Ella's nice sheets, the galloping stead was yanking some lose, the bucket headed boy tossing side to side was dislodging others blowing some now completely afield, some ripped over the barbed wire fence, a few pillow slips were kiting along the red dirt road.

Homer disappeared from sight. Mrs. Ella and Pete appeared on sight. They got a dazed N.L. down off his horse and the pot off his head. Dreams of roundtable knighthood banished forever, N.L. was racked to the stake of hand washing all those sheets and Tobe was retired to field duty.

Years later N.L. as the now Dr. Tim McLeod in Austin, Texas would run again as a knight- this was with the McCallum High School Knights when he charged ahead of the team coming on the field with staff and banner. This time it actually was to the cheers of supporting fans and no team ever caught up with the galloping McCallum Knight Dr N.L..Tim McLeod. Esq.

N.L.'s Rain Fire

In the dust bowl of the late 1920's early 1930's mid-America had some blackout days but on CatClaw Creek it was just another blustery time of blowing fine red dust. It could get so dusky even at noon car lights had to be turned on as one had to feel braille like one's way down the road.

Back to back dust storms are fairly normal to everyone in Trent. N.L. would go to school wiping off a fairy layer of rusty granules from his desk. At home in his loft he could feel tiny flecks sifting through the cracks and if he shook out his blanket a small crimson cloud for a moment hung in the air. He watched his Mama, Mrs. Ella tirelessly fight the gritty invasion sweeping/mopping floors, porches, even the hard-pan packed grassless yard-one tiny broom against this monsoon of red.

N.L. pondered the 'what ifs?' cause something had to be done. Perhaps the rainmakers, the climate charlatans, wizards of the weather had it all wrong with their provoking pyro tactics like it was the 4th of July. Maybe God's nature needed only a gentle nudge, as he had read in King Arthur in Camelot it could never rain till after sundown. Maybe it was in this medieval plan that this modern-evil question could find an answer.

With the help of Homer at first, who soon quit the job for lack of inspiration N.L. rescued an old bathing tub from a garbage heap. He sat it up on blocks and plugged up the drain hole. He reasoned what the skies needed (like yeast) was a small gentle starter batch of evaporated water.

He would fill the tub with well-water burning wood underneath and - viola! Moisture sky ascending soon to be recycled as dust settling big fat rain droplets- it was worthy of 'try'.

With Pete's permission (if he chopped the wood himself) N.L. hauled water and wood to his tub which he had set up behind the barn where the pasture starts. His small fires and the dry heat keep him going back for more well water. The smallest cotton cloud brush stroked over prevailing blue was inspiring enough to keep small bubbles of hope streaming up in the tub and heart.

One evening the plot had played out long enough that this was going to be his bust or dust finale. He built using all his left over wood a handsome fire and had plenty of well water therein before going to bed. No one knew for sure exactly what happened next. At sunrise next door down the road neighbor Mr. Nabor came knocking 'I be missing one of my ewe's had them herded up next to the barn but can't find her anywhere-hide nor hair!' He told Mr. Pete he had heard yelps and barkings and that maybe a pack of wild dogs went through. Mr. Pete thanked him and said they would be on the lookout.

What truly happened was never witnessed so surmised

summations built the story. Maybe the ewe got out on her own just as the dogs came along. There was a helter-skelter chase.

Perhaps terrorized by the tooth and claw that ewe tried to evade their jaws by doing the unthinkable being just nipped from behind she had jumped!- maybe to go over the tub but she did not make it. She went into the tub! Her hoofs gained no traction in the tub for escape. For there she was found that morning boiled in N.L.'s rainmaking machine. The Nabors and the McLeods were thunderstruck (not in the way N.L. had hoped for) as N.L. explained it was certainly not his intention to cook off in sacrifice his neighbors lamb.

Making the best of boiling, they skinned the sacrificial lamb and the tenderized meat was enough for a two family feast! From this humble beginning N.L. completely gave up rain-making and became instead a BarBQer extraordinary. Later in life on his Small Fry Ranch in south Travis County he would have his own grill pit in a BarBQ house- fire stall, rack, chimney, sink and cabinets. To this day those who had the pleasure of his smoked offering raise a camp-cook salute to the God's of grilling that there was none was better. He tendered fixings for family, friends, churches, even an entire 9th grade Lamar Scottie football team. He would remind them all that an open fire pit can get your goat! Or also chicken, pork, steak, even fish and one can become a charcoal commander.

Printed in the United States
by Baker & Taylor Publisher Services